THE LUCKIEST ST. PATRICK'S DAY EVER!

THE LUCKIEST ST. PATRICK'S DAY EVER!

BY **TEDDY SLATER**

ILLUSTRATED BY **ETHAN LONG**

SCHOLASTIC INC.

NEW YORK   TORONTO   LONDON   AUCKLAND   SYDNEY

MEXICO CITY   NEW DELHI   HONG KONG   BUENOS AIRES

ISBN-13: 978-0-545-03943-7
ISBN-10: 0-545-03943-6

10 9 8 7 6 5   10 11 12/0
Printed in the U.S.A.
First printing, February 2008

Top o' the morning!
It's March seventeen.
The Leprechaun family
is wearing the green.

St. Patrick's parade
is about to begin.
The wee ones are marching.
Come on—let's join in!

There goes Bedelia, leading the clan,
arm in arm with Granddaddy Dan.
She swings her shillelagh.
They walk and talk gaily,
moving as fast as they can.

Timothy Shaunnessy,
handsome and bold,
marches along
with a big pot of gold.

And here comes Aunt Rose,
tap-tapping her toes.
With shamrock in hand,
she follows the band,
decked out in her very best clothes.

Tootle-dee-toot!
Rum-a-tum-tum!
Johnny and Jack play the fife and the drum.

They kick up their heels
in a wild Irish jig.
Everyone's dancing...
even the pig!

After the march,
it's back home for lunch...
mulligan stew and
green apple punch.

Kate cuts the cabbage.
Pat shells the peas.
The mischievous children
do just as they please.

Friends and family keep coming to call.
There's plenty of food for one and for all.

The Caseys, MacGregors, O'Gradys, Peg Finn.
Everyone's welcome—please, won't you come in!

Lassies and laddies
stream through the door,
until there's no room
for one caller more.

The Leprechauns crowd
'round the dining-room table,

piling their plates as high as they're able.

But before they dig in,
they have one thing to say,

"May the luck of the Irish
be with you today!"